Scarlet Fan

by Melody Lemond

To order additional copies of this book, contact:
Xlibris
1-800-455-039
www.xlibris.com.au
Orders@Xlibris.com.au

FOREWORD

Scarlet Fan was conceived as a result of a desire on my part, many years ago now, to create a dance-theatre spectacle. I was riding on the inspiration of truly great theatre, vis. the Lindsay Kemp Company, with which I travelled for a year during their stay in Australia in 1974—and the following year, of Marcel Marceau, with whom I shared a powerful and 'intimately universal' bond where, through the dark of the theatre, subtle psychic emanations were co-transmitted on 'levels' too fine to otherwise express. Fuelling this desire was my notion then that such states of shared delight ought not, ideally speaking, be contained within the physical, albeit sanctioned frame of theatre. And so I set myself the deliberate 'artistic challenge' of allowing it to flow beyond the construct of its four walls, beyond time and space. Idealism at its most naive, perhaps, yet I felt impelled.

And so for seven years I sent him, Marceau (who was at the time the knight in this story), 'every flower and thing of beauty' (Philomena), in the meantime co-channelling a compilation of 'words from the gods', with the intention of it resulting in a finished product adaptable to theatre. A short cut, perhaps. Also, and no less importantly to me, it was a way of maintaining contact with Marceau (for whom this artistic challenge was not shared; not in keeping with his own intentions). The channelling sessions, held each month during the rise of the moon for about a year (and which I sent to Marceau each month in the form of letters), comprised considerable guidance from beings who were happy to comply with my request: to present themselves as mythical gods. Interspersed among the chapters were also conversations in simple French with Marceau from wherever he was in the world. When he returned on his next tour seven years later (by which time the magic of my challenge showed itself to be no longer sustainable), Marceau corrected, during a couple of our meetings, those French passages. That compendium, 'Crystal Fragments', no longer exists.

Prior to my dispersing it among friends, however, I decided to embark on the task of selecting from it some segments which might lend themselves to a possible story that I might ultimately use as a theatre script. It was not feasible to create at this stage of my life a theatre production such as I had been guided to do—not to mention with myself performing as Philomena, whose role I found myself playing in the channelled book to maintain the dialogue. It did occur to me momentarily, though, perhaps part subconsciously, that I might at some stage ere long bear a child, a daughter who might wish to be a dancer and who might, perhaps, harbour among her own dream-plans, a wish to perform this role.

I did give birth to a son, now a scientist and an avid surfer; and to a daughter, now a talented dancer and choreographer. It is to them both, Jeremy and Angela, that I lovingly dedicate this book. Despite its long and arduous period of labour, I am comforted with the knowledge that its birth is timely, and that it will show itself to be a product that will touch widely.

4

There was a time, not long before the dawning of this age, when little seemed to shine upon the planet Terra, as it was then so aptly named. Naught but the flash and flicker of a flame here and there, shooting sparks from the dim, desert abyss.

Erratic sparks of hope, such as we see emanate from this lone flameflower, as she opens her petals to greet the coming day. Filled is this flower with the fire of feeling—with the fullness of joy in all its fragrance—and with the force of sorrow when her love is withheld. But what an amazing flower! Its petals are concentric rings of fire continually expanding and growing with new rings, always being formed at the centre, pushing its outer orbit even farther into the reaches of space and time. The centre is a flaming hub of activity. Oh fiery flower, how do you grow? You are beautiful, fiery flower, but if your growth remains unchecked, uncontrolled, how can you see where you are growing? Who is at your centre to guide you? Where are your farthest petals bound, fiery-petalled flower? What can sustain them? For, fiery flower, you know they need something to cling to. Are all your petals still in touch? As long as they continue to shine, then they must be. . . So who stokes your furnace, fiery flower? Who makes you shine so bright, sending orbs of coloured flame wheeling through the night? Unpredictable are the moods of nature. A sudden gust of wind and—yes! One of the petals has taken off. It is as though she is wanting to forge a new life for herself. Or perhaps, it was her mother-flower, so deeply rooted to her spot on the earth, who let her go, thus to ensure the fulfilment of her own dreams. The petal was carried into the air, floating flake-like through the azure sky. And it was with the birds which hovered above and about her that she felt a strange kinship. They seemed to rejoice in her newfound freedom and chirped merrily as they led her far from her desert homeland towards more fertile coastal regions. It was here that the fresh green earth below invited her to land. And for many a timeless moment she lay, gazing in wonderment at her new surroundings. She felt so small amidst the tall woodland pines. Yet, pondering her past where she was fixed to the ground by a stem, she felt a strong desire to flutter forth freely and explore her new environment. But the wind which had so bountifully borne her was gone, and she was unable to move.

Perhaps… No! She could not go back now.

At last, with an imploring gaze, she looked up to the timely appearance of a magnificently, multi-coloured angel-bird. 'Come here!' he said. 'Dance with me. Leave all past cares behind. Don't worry about your fellow petals, the companions you left behind. Duty to yourself is foremost and beautiful.' 'And who are you?' cried the petal in surprise. 'I'm a dancer,' replied the angel-bird, spreading his beautiful rainbow wings. 'You too would wish to be a bird. But a bird who cannot fly isn't one. You must turn your vision into something all can see.

6

Only then can the caged bird be set free.' 'But how?' asked the petal, timidly. 'My vision is locked inside and I am unable to move.' 'Start by flapping your wings,' said the angel-bird. 'That generates enough energy to start with. All good dancers flap their wings daily and sparrows start at the crack of dawn. They wake the world with their song and beating of wings. Even though they are often at risk, the joy of flight makes it all worthwhile. 'You see your world within your grasp; to be there is another thing. 'A bird looks out upon the skies; 'tis not the same as taking wing. 'Birds are lucky. They had good parents who fed them and kept them warm and made them sing for their supper. Taught them to fly before they could walk and pushed them from the nest in full flight. To fly and to sing and to nest, to hunt for one's food, to form beautiful patterns in the sky: these are what a bird needs. 'A bird is rarely still, lost or unhappy. Its feelings are in its wings and throat. 'The sombre earthbound birds don't count. The lyrebird may be pretty, but it lacks the joy of high flight.'

'But what makes birds fly?' asked the petal coyly. 'Well', said the angel-bird, 'they must fly, they must sing because it is their nature and therefore they're given the energy to do it. If you are as hungry as they, you too will have the urge to continue. Their secret is a sense of purpose. They are following a star.' The petal looked up just in time to see a huge black eagle flying up to the sun. 'That's all right', assured the angel-bird, following the petal's gaze. 'Eagles can fly up to the sun. They don't get their wings singed. High-flying fiery hybrid. It loves its nest when day is done, but all alone must it fly across the sun. The eagle pounces on its prey. Do or be done to! 'Those who don't aim for the stars become creatures of fate and are pounced on by those who do. 'Victims set their sights too low. High-flying birds are above such matters. When one flies high, mundane concerns look after themselves. One will always be provided for when one aims for the stars.'

'But a star is so very far,' exclaimed the petal, despondently. 'If I'm to win, then where do I begin?'

'Start by flapping your wings', gestured the angel-bird, 'and warbling a few notes in the mornings. Concentrate on one thing at a time and make sure it's important. The rest doesn't matter. Then your wings will take you towards the star you have your sight set on. Find your star, the sooner the better.'

'But how?' asked the little petal.

'You know what birds do', said the angel-bird. 'It's as simple as that!' And with that, he flew off.

The petal was left feeling astounded, gazing at the space which the extraordinary bird had traced. 'How awesome is beauty sometimes', she thought. 'Would that I were so splendid. Would that I could fly so free.'

'But you aaare freee', whispered the wakening wind. 'You aaaaarrrrre frreeeeee.'

With a gentle touch, he planted a network of veins into her soft velvet body and breathed upon it little wing-shaped limbs. Delighted at this change, she stood, then began to wave them.

Her movements, though hesitant at first, grew surer as she imitated the flight of the birds. Philomena skipped excitedly through the trees, flapping her arms about, moving her delicate green fingers and bowing and stretching like the branches above.

After awhile, feeling a little tired, she sat by a tree and began to ponder the mysteries of life. As the sun was sinking through the trees, the birds ceased their chirping and all was still and hushed. Yet no sooner had this silence reached her, than there came to her ears the faint sounds of what seemed to be a horse in gallop. The sounds grew louder and slower as it approached. And then she saw it, so clear against the dimming light: a brilliant white horse and upon it a knight. He was clad in a white velvet suit, richly embroidered in braidings of bronze. His face was hidden behind the visor of his helmet, which he now removed, holding it to his chest. His eyes met hers and upon them dwelt. 'Fear not, Philomena', he said, 'for our lives and our dreams can now be as one. Indeed, long, long ago, our very souls were as one and we were complete. But the trials of time have separated us and only now are we free to reap the fruits of justice.' It was the first time Philomena had heard her name. This name, though new to her, sounded sweet to her ear and strangely familiar. 'Who are you?' cried Philomena. 'And. . . who am I?'

'My name is Will', said the night. 'I am fire and you are water.'

'But – I'm born of a flameflower. How can I be water?' asked Philomena.

'We're all born of a flame', said the knight. 'And within us all glows a spark from that flame. It is the eternal spark of our essence. But also within us all are complementary opposites which must co-exist in perfect balance—within male, within female. The sun is fire; the moon, water. Somehow the two must meet. But the fire must not turn water to steam, nor must water quench the fire. Intuition comes first—from the water. With the marriage of sun and moon, fire and water, we will again be complete—together, forever.'

Jumping from his horse, the knight's eyes fixed on Philomena's. Then he knelt before her, lifted her little hands into his and gently urged: 'Simply focus on the theatre of your mind. Let the players appear. Let them do what they will. For they will guide us to the source of our yearnings and pour their blessings through us upon the world. 'My spirit shall not be far from you.' He smiled, pressing into her palm a little gift. It was a fan-shaped brooch of scarlet and silver with two dancing figures engraved upon it. 'We shall be as one again,' he promised. So touched was Philomena that she held it to her heart, into which it fused. 'Farewell, Philomena,' cried the knight, his starry eyes touching her depths. Then mounting his steed, he put on his helmet and galloped off through the woods.

Philomena was puzzled. She felt exhilarated, and yet at the same time, sad and confused. For certain feelings, long dormant, were welling up within her. Her self-questionings were irrepressible, coming, it seemed, from the deepest recesses of her heart. It was as though something deep, deep inside her had just been re-awakened.

'Why', she asked herself, 'was I born a mere petal, when I want so much to be other things as well? What is it that motivates me, of all petals, to feel this strange desire? To soar through the boundaries of form to realms beyond even my own imaginings? And, what is it all about, this meeting with the knight?

'The wind can surely see my plight, for it gave me limbs to aid my flight. Yet it whispers secrets I don't understand. Secrets of some quest that's right and grand. But what is this quest? What lies at its end? 'Ah. . . memories so dim of seasons forgotten, where the flowers and fruits can never go rotten, where the rose no longer needs its thorn—and hearts can never ever be torn. Here, I'm sure, there can be no end. . . nor even a beginning! Oh. . . I don't comprehend. The seasons have cycles. Their moods are many. No, there is no end. How could there be any? 'But I'm getting lost now in my mind's own maze. I think I'll just rest on this boulder—and gaze.' So Philomena sat and watched the forest throw shadows as it was stripped of its day-dress. And no longer was she chained by her thoughts. Her attention now turned to the sky whose colours were quickly changing from gold to orange and purple as the sun was setting.

'How subtle is this change from day to night', she thought, as she watched the hues of mauve mingling and merging with pastels of pink. 'If I stop to reflect even for a moment, then it seems I miss the next!' she exclaimed. 'Beauty may be awesome, but—it's also very fleeting. Why, I can barely capture it.' Philomena's gaze was sad as the sky turned to indigo blue and was studded with stars. 'There must be millions!' she thought, as she tried to count them. 'Seventy-six, seventy-seven, seventy. . . but. . . what is this?' she exclaimed. 'It is clearly not a star.'

And neither was it. For as it drew near, it assumed the form of a shining chariot, which landed right in front of her. And lo! Alighting from it gracefully was a lady so exquisite in every detail that Philomena stood mesmerized.

The lady was youthful and of indeterminate age. Yet there was an incongruous blend of worldliness, innocence, wisdom, benevolence, and a knowledge of things secret in her demeanour. One noticed first her aura of shimmering rainbow colours, blending into dazzling white. Her hair was like spun-gold and seemed endless. It was caught up in braids and pinned with precious stones. The long cascades of these undulating tresses fell in delightful abandon.

Her face was alabaster white and translucent, as though carved of fine marble, as Pygmalion did Galatea. Her eyes were large and lustrous. But what fascinated most about them was their colour, which was ever-changing. Now grey. . . now smoky. . . now sapphire blue – next, the turgid green of a turbulent sea. . . and sometimes smouldering black, but above all, clear–crystal clear. Her eyes were like two crystals in which might be seen anything reflected one cared to know. She was wearing a gown of emerald green, and upon her head a diamond crown, for this, indeed, was Venus the queen. And she spoke:

'A moon–kissed daydream is a wondrous thing. From such dreams star-crossed lovers spring. Stars pulsate, sending glittering spangles to drench the world in their light. Centres of gentle energy pulsate. Quiescent thought-beams take flight. 'When the moon's a silver sliver, she's to hang your dreams upon—to give them time to ripen when the splendour's fully shone. 'Don't think she's not with you when she turns her back away. Just call her out of hiding and she'll be there, come what may.'

'Who are you?' asked Philomena in wonderment.

'One of the frantic ones who wants to see more action.'

'Action?' queried Philomena, looking concerned.

'Yes, from the within to the without, in one way or another. You'll see. Ever–so–wondrous are the night's delights for those who have had an active day, while those who sit at home alone reap nothing from their idle play.'

'And what of a star alone in the sky?' asked Philomena. 'How does it act?' 'Revolving planets have their courses marked by time and space, for each and every one knows it will show its shining face.' 'But will it see other shining faces? And if so, is that doing nothing?' Philomena asked, plaintively.

And again, the queen replied softly: 'A star is a star when seen from afar. How do you know you're not a star to someone else from whom you are far, yet able still to shine your light and send off sparks to his midnight?'

'I'm clothed in flesh and my wings are not yet formed,' cried Philomena. 'How can I do more?'

'Bodies of light can shine', said the queen, 'as temples for the soul divine. And when this we undergo, through the world our light can flow. Look at the moon!' she said, pointing up at the pearly white opal. 'Her shine comes from the sun. Even when he's gone away, his image she holds in store.'

Once again, the golden face of the knight, glowing ethereal, was mirrored in Philomena's mind. And in the vividness of this moment, she realized that her yearnings for him were from a time long, long before their recent encounter. A flurry of images swept through her being, images of herself as a maiden, waiting, hoping through many a waxing moon—and weeping, weeping at their wane.

Ah, the moon! How she had loved the moon, breathed the moon. Yet how sad it had sometimes seemed—and pale like a camellia, as though forlorn and anguished, starkly suspended in a fathomless sky. Memories only of the waning . . . waning memories . . .

'From shine to shine the arrows whirl,' continued the queen. 'The moonbeam travels on from place to place through time and space, never lingering long. Always on the move, she flows with magic, dance, and song, transferring all her energy around and back again. She needs her audience, the moon. For her, to shine is life. But also does she need the sun, for she is his wife. 'And we are all so like her in each and every way. We always know that we can go. We know we cannot stay. Why try and fight the urge to flight? The real stars never do. They travel on throughout the night and love the day so blue.' 'Don't they ever stop?' asked Philomena. 'Their flight is endless through the sky's vast lake, though they may well pause for a moment to make.' '. . . and share?' 'And then they charge on when the moment's gone, for others are waiting there. They pause in their flight to exchange their light with other travelling stars for whom they parade in a showering cascade of delight.' 'Delight. . . ,' sighed Philomena despondently. 'That's something I've long been without. It's a state I've known, but now I doubt.' As soon as this last word was uttered, the queen mounted her chariot, saying: 'The moment you doubt I must disappear. But I promise your every call I shall hear.' She was lifted off in her chariot, and all that was left was a trail of broken light which fizzled at Philomena's feet.

'But how, after all this time, can I help but doubt?' thought Philomena, as her sadness surged up and o'er-whelmed her. 'All I've seen, touched, and felt I've sent him, every moment of every day—every flower and thing of beauty. Must I, like them, just fade away? How can I know that he shares these treasures, or feels these joys, these 'mutual' pleasures? If to doubt is to die, then die I must. For I see no tangible sign of tr—'. There came, then, a flash of lightning so bright that it shocked her, sending tremors through her being as she looked up in terror. And there, on the threshold of his shining domain, heralded by the stroke of lightning, stood Mars. He was garbed in a long red robe, trimmed with gold. And his foreboding countenance caused Philomena to quiver a little as she greeted him politely. 'H-how do you do?' Mars' tone was very firm as he replied: 'That depends on the needs of the time. One can have enough of peace! There comes a time when it is right to imitate the action of a tiger! 'Sometimes there's a lot of debris to be cleared away, and then they ring me up and say: "Mars—there's work for you today!" 'They speak of me behind my back and say I cause all wars and strife! Oh yes, they paint me pretty black. But if you don't know death you don't know life! 'And so, I even up the score. In my own way I balance out. Where once was less, I make it more. They don't know what I'm about.'

'How do you make it more?' asked Philomena.

'I raise the nerves in everyone. I set them on their mark. It's such a shame that only war can kindle up that spark! It seems so self-destructive that all they can think to do is stamp around and kill themselves instead of. . . making something new. For this is not what I would have them do with their ferocious ways. They could be turned to good account and man could see more vibrant days—within his lifetime too, if he could only change his tune. You'll be hearing from me soon.'

And with another lightning flash, followed by a tremendous thunderclap, Mars disappeared.

Philomena was exasperated. The mere thought of war, or of any disruption to the harmony she saw, made her own sadness seem petty. For war is surely not very pretty.

'There must be no war!' she exclaimed aloud, her eyes piercing the skies.

'War is simply action misdirected,' said an owl from a nearby branch, his form silhouetted against the moon. 'There must be no war, but there must be action. It is only when man's dreams are frustrated and neglected that he turns towards such destructive things. But if he dwells on the high, noble, and pure things in life, his dreams will be nourished.

Yet to externalize them, he needs the fire and drive of the Mars temperament. When this applied to noble goals, then no harm is done. 'Follow the light. Remember always that the powers of light are stronger than the powers of darkness. 'Love and do what thou wilt. Do it! If you are loving, then whatever you do cannot be wrong. If more people knew this, the world would be full of positive vibrations, distilled in an essence of love—love, light and energy.' Then, with a gentle, reassuring voice, he blinked his big bright eyes and said: 'Mars means no harm. His ways may seem wicked, but he really only wants to wake people up. And sometimes, when they don't move, he has to scare them into life with wars. Mars loves action and energy. But where he sees an idle force field, he must meddle. For such lifelessness is not allowed in nature. Remember this and all will be well. The point is to keep moving—in one's soul, in one's body—movement is of the essence. The problems of the world come to land on the shoulders of those who stagnate because they are standing there to receive them. If you're as light as a feather, nimble and quick and slippery like a fish, you can dart past the teeth of sharks and come to no harm. You can reap good everywhere you go, tapping beneficence from on high and showering the world with glad tidings. Take heart at this and keep busy.'

As though to confirm his wise words, the owl swooped down and, flapping his wings wildly, winked at Philomena and flew off into the night. 'Well', thought Philomena, 'life must be very simple if all I must do is love and keep moving. Moving. . . action. . . Oh, it seems there's much to do. . . and so, so little time. . . But for now. . . I think I'll just sleep. . . and dream.' And dream she did till dawn roused her. She yawned and stretched and set off for a leisurely walk. And, to her amazement, she saw that the woods were being painted rosy pink by the delicate brushstrokes of dawn. And as she ambled along, clusters of morning glories opened their arms of lilac. Indeed, one by one, all the flowers greeted her, waiting to catch the drops of dew, drink enough on a morning so new.

Her woodland home was sprinkled with colour. The stream was gurgling as it trickled by, and the birds sang happily as she wandered up the slopes.

And there, on a hilltop before her, stood a figure so handsome, so splendid against the brightening sky that Philomena was both motionless and speechless. He was carrying a golden sundial, which he now held out before her. 'I wonder who this could be!' thought Philomena. His mouth, as it opened, looked like a poised bow and his voice was strong and clear. 'I am one of the gods of Time,' he announced. 'If you knew my nature better, I could not limit you. Eternity is not so far away, but it's hard to see the light of day when Saturn's rings constrict and bind. Then inner space is hard to find. 'Those who feel themselves my slaves should step back just a pace or two. Then they'd see that all they crave lies in another point of view.' 'Mmm,' thought Philomena, tilting her head sideways. 'There may be some truth in this.'

18

'Listen!' he commanded. 'Do you hear the music of silence?' Philomena put her hand to her ear, listening. . . listening. . . and lo!

Wild creatures are dancing in the woods. Like furies from Ancient Greece they hurl themselves, whirling human torches of ecstasy and lust. They are dancing to unheard music, for the pipes of Pan are beyond mortal ears.

Dionysus has set his men to catch them, for here the Rites of Spring know no bounds. The women are wild. Their hair flies. Their arms and legs are thrown askew like gnarled oak trees. They wear green tattered garments which rustle in the wind and their feet beat a pounding rhythm in harmony with the tempo of earth. This creates a hypnotic drumming effect which keeps the dance continuing and leads it on to its final crescendo. Philomena is sent awhirl with the force of the dance, till, at the point of climax she is left twirling at the centre, whilst the others thread around her. Weaving lyrically through the dull thudding of bare feet on bare earth comes the silvery serpentine song of a rare nightingale—a bird of paradise indeed. And from on high, lifting the song to alternate peaks and undulating troughs of cadence and contrast, come piercing jets of white sound, shooting high into the stars from the base of the beating of drums. It is like a high-pitched flute—for divine ears only. Some of the women leave the earth and are transported through the air, weaving a sympathetic dance to the mimed melancholy of the cypress and cedars, while others float golden in the glorious light of the sun, suspended in an amber ether between heaven and earth. The silver and the gold thread around and through and between and below and above each other in perfect harmony. It is a festival of goddesses, moving in response to unheard music, unheard, at least, to mortal ears. Philomena continued to spin, around and around and around in the centre. . . or is she the centre? It is like the dance of the whirling dervish, seemingly endless. And when the festival had finished, Philomena, as she span, could hear its echo—whispers reverberating, it seemed, from the dancers themselves: 'When we reach the peaks of musical possibility we find we can go higher still,' said one.

'Once we have transcended the narrow boundaries of what is thought possible, there is no limit,' said another.

Then came a chorus of whispers. 'When we stay close to our own true nature, we may harmonize with others who do likewise, though there may be worlds of difference between us. 'Those of us who stamp out the rhythms of the earth in wild abandon express ourselves fully. 'We stamp out patterns in the cosmos, just as those who make music in more ethereal realms likewise trace through space, creating cosmic spider webs of pure and ethereal sound. 'Each of us is true to her own nature and, thus, becomes perfect in what she is.

'Music belongs to the world of the wondrous. And when we vibrate in harmony to cosmic rhythms and melodies, we become more than we think we are. For thus we draw down the power of the gods and become one with the golden chain of our good. 'An entry into the world of aesthetics is a doorway to another dimension where the confines of narrow egotism, habits, and opinions are seen for what they are—as if from a great distance—and thus dissolve and faade awaaay. . .' So with the approach of dusk, did the chorus fade, and Philomena's spinning slowed to an ebb.

Her limbs were failing her, so she lay down on the grass and gazed at the expanses above— elated, content. But the longer she gazed, the more her contentment became usurped by a state of quandary. Time. . . timelessness. . . images of women who had welcomed her into their silent world of ritual.

'Those moments so magical were real. Real! I was there. I took part. Yet, it's as though it all happened in a moment, a moment out of time. . . beyond time. . . through the split of a moment! 'It may have been the moment before this, it may have been yesterday, it may have been seasons ago. Whichever the moment, I was there. I was part of that magical scene. 'And oh, what joy! But he will never know. Never. How to describe it to the knight? 'How to describe what can only be transmitted at the same moment? 'Oh, why, why couldn't he have been there… to catch me in his arms and share my delight? Why?'

Philomena now began to wonder if all her strange adventures, peculiar to herself, were real. 'Are all these heavenly helpers real? Am I? Is the knight? 'Yes, he must certainly be real, for he gave me this heart-brooch… but he did promise we'd be together at last and. . . it's now been several cycles since he left. Why did he leave?

'Oh, I feel so cold. . . so cold. . . The winter trees are stripped of their glory and all is stark and bare. 'The birds no longer sing their merry song. No longer do I see them fly. And, if they don't, then, how can I? 'Movement. . . goals so elusive. . . how can I continue? No longer can my purpose move me, or I with it.' Philomena huddled on the grass, shivering.

Perhaps, if a glimmer of hope remained, it was this that raised her sad little face to the skies, as though magnetically drawn to a single star, a twinkling red star.

Then, Philomena recognized a voice, though it was now more gentle. 'I am the benevolent aspect of Mars. Are you losing heart? Do you not comprehend the role of winter? It is a receptive time; a time for reflection, for introspection. A time for integration. It has its season. It has its place. 'But be not mistaken, there is movement in the chill. It is not a time to stop, to give in, or give up. Soon the trees will show their green again.

Another spring—another surge, outwards and onwards. There will be a time to bring your fruits to light, to see your newborn dreams take flight when the time is right to let your spirit soar. But first you must learn some more. 'A dream is a dream is a dream. But sometimes, held too long inside, they can pile up until the soul cries out, "Enough!" Then it's time to send them into the light of day and give them form and meaning to sustain them on their way, that they may live forever in the hearts of those they may impress with their beauty and truthfulness. 'But with no action, nothing can transpire, and sometimes to get things moving, it takes fire. I will admit some overdo it here. Their wells run dry and all they touch they sear. 'They are the arid ones, the desert souls. They are afraid of water and its goals. But you are not like that. In fact, a little fire will do no harm at all. Without its balance, you could well fall. 'Both fire and water must be well controlled to be put to good use, for I'm told that each in excess can destroy the world.

'I have come because you need me to externalize your dreams. I do not wish to destroy them, or you, or anyone. It's those with little insight who do that. They destroy themselves by abusing my powers and scorch their very souls. 'Alas, but the balance must always work out in one way or another. 'And now you know enough, I feel, to go and make your dreams come real. 'So keep on shining bright and hold fast to the ribbon of light. I wish to see you live your story and rise up in a blaze of glory, for this is where I reside and seek to seduce the ones who hide, afraid to show their light, afraid that I might bite. I do not have to do that. Their fears do it for me. 'Yet those who are beings of light will find that all the world is a spot-lit stage. 'And now I must away, but I've just this to say: 'Don't keep your dreams in hiding, but be brave—and alert to the help of others on your wave, for many a familiar or unknown face is the mask of some god, your will to brace. 'So fear not, for fate will lend a helping hand, and you shall both shine in the Promised Land.'

No sooner had Philomena begun to wonder as to the nature of this 'Promised Land' than the twinkling red star disappeared, behind a cloud perhaps. 'I shall heed your every word!' proclaimed Philomena. And as she rose to her feet, she felt a strange warmth in her belly. It was the fire of will, of determination. She strode along the grassy slopes till she arrived at what seemed to be a stream, for she could faintly hear the sound of water trickling, and her feet were slightly damp.

Carefully she felt her way to a grassy clearing, edging herself as close to the stream as possible, close enough for her to peer into the water's depths, the depths of her being. 'A time for reflection... ' she recalled. Her thoughts, as she looked into the dark waters, were many. So many. So much to integrate. Philomena remembered every word uttered to her by each of her visiting friends—words of hope, encouragement, wisdom.

And upon each word she reflected. Long and hard she thought... until her mind became so clouded that all she could do was cry out: 'Where is he? Where is he?' into the dark stream. It caught a tear as it flurried past... and another... yet it made no reply. Philomena, in the grip of her anguish, clenched her little fists, tightened her little body and let herself scream: 'Help me shine my light through the night! Help me!' And the stream answered with a shine, reflecting as it flowed, a tortured face—an expression which softened as the image of a star shone brightly upon and through her.

Beside the star, reflected in the stream, was a shimmering crescent moon.

Philomena, recognizing another voice, glanced up to see Venus shining through the clouds. 'I've come in answer to your plaintive plea, the crescent moon accompanying me. 'Imagination,' she said. 'It's imagination that chains us... and it's imagination that sets us free. 'All the stars had to go through this lonely process of agony and alienation. That is why they call the night an anguish-woven tapestry. But shine, little star. Be gentle with yourself. 'There need be no effort. Simply shine.' 'Oh... where is he? Will he see my shine? Where is the knight?' 'You fear he's gone, your white-light knight... Has it not occurred to you that he may also be waiting... hoping? Long has he waited... and still he waits. Yet in his waiting there is movement; he is not passive, but receptive. But he too becomes impatient now, restless. So he's leaving the pleasant green meadow for harsh and rugged terrain, for there's no place for a knight in a meadow. Sheep belong in meadows. 'He needs the ups and downs, the highs and lows, to be himself. It will be hard but the rewards will be great. Besides, there's someone he's looking for. 'He needs her as she needs him. He needs some of her softness as she needs some of his strength. He must find her, else his ferocious energy will turn in upon itself and cause his destruction. 'And so must she meet him, for she and he are one. Without her he is merely blind force, and without him she's an ineffectual weakling, a dreamer. 'He needs her inspiration to give direction to his energy and fire. She needs his strength to give structure to her wishful daydreams. He is looking for his soul, and she is looking for recognition. 'This is why they are fatally attracted and why neither can survive without the other and why all would do well to cultivate the qualities of each within themselves so that a race of divine androgens may arise and all may have the strength and sensitivity, action, and introspection, going out and coming in, yang and yin—all in the one being. 'That is what we are all working on right now. This is the formula for externalizing our dreams, and this is why we cannot underestimate the importance of meetings.' 'Is the knight a god?' asked Philomena. 'When alone he is a warrior unleashed on a battlefield, but when his fierce and fiery ways are directed and inspired by intuition, he can achieve great creative ends. But he can be destructive when his fire gets out of control, when he lacks balance. 'Certainly it cannot be argued that he has force. Yet whether results will be positive or negative depends on how it's directed. He must be inspired before he blazes forth, else his energy will be wasted. 'The sun and moon must be in balance. Each must harmonize with the other for successful fruits of this union.'

'I cannot see him as destructive,' retorted Philomena. 'The knight—in his pure and primeval sense—is magnificent. But he's like a loaded gun that needs to be pointed somewhere and set off. When his sights are set on a particular goal his energies are in control, but when they scatter he burns himself up with solatic power. He just needs a little inner direction to turn his tremendous force into a creative one. Yes, the warrior and the enchantress must meet and as one divinely androgynous being will reap great changes and influence all humanity.' 'How will they meet?' asked Philomena. 'When the time is right and the balanced opposing forces are in harmony, moments in time will sparkle and will be a sublimely, supremely important series of nows or happenings, sequences, chains of events.' Philomena, her eyes still fixed on the star, raised her little hand to the brooch embedded in her heart, noticing as she did, that the voice of Venus was receding as the clouds blocked her light. Then, for a fleeting moment, she was once more visible—a pinpoint of light, and beside her, the crescent moon. The familiar voice, now barely audible, continued: 'As roses kiss Summer and seas swell to greet, in full moon momentum merging minds meet. Look now, beyond tomorrow, at the point where joy meets sorrow. It's here that your friends reside in this anguish-woven tapestry, side by side.

'Philomena watched as the star became enveloped by the cumulus clouds. 'So, even in sorrow there's movement', she mused, feeling some comfort in her sadness. 'Even as this storm rages, tossing its troth about skies, so must I move now. For I know no other way. The storm, as my sorrow doesn't abate. Yet it moves— and I with it. It will pass. The skies will clear… and the time will be right when I see the knight.' Philomena, in her fortitude, let herself cry. The sound of her sobs was drowned by the thunder and her tears mingled with the rain as it now pelted down. She was submerged in her sorrow—the deepest sorrow, turning now into despair: a state she knew she must avoid. So, seizing the moment, she clutched her scarlet-jewelled heart to press away the pain. Yet still the tears would not cease and she could not quell the sobs—no more than the rolls of thunder. Her gaze now shifted back to the skies. The clouds were parting to reveal a ceiling of stars, blazing through the blanket of rain. 'So many friends . . .' she whispered to herself. Then, in a broken, choking voice, she said: 'How, oh how, can I ever reach them? So many words of strength-giving comfort yet—how can I be deserving of them? Oh stars, my friends, if only through my sadness I could reach you! If even through sorrow my light could touch . . .' Suddenly one star intensified its light and pulsated as it spoke through the teaming rain. 'All of nature cries out for more water. When the cups run over, the rocks of the desert shall erode. Fire shall smoulder and swords of steel shall find no resistance.'

Philomena, rubbing her eyes, sprang from her bed of grass and cried: 'Who is this?' 'I am the star of hope, the Waterbearer. I radiate my light for all who care to see. Water offers no resistance. It ebbs and flows according to the forces acting on it at the time. It is the strongest of the elements. For it is boundless and limitless and flows sympathetic to the temporary boundaries which guide it unerringly towards the sea, which is where it longs to be.

Now the fiery temperament prevails and the imbalance is dangerous to the extreme. Yet water can overcome it if allowed to. That is why we must allow water-consciousness to flood the arid deserts of our own making. The fertile waters of the subconscious mind must be allowed to trickle out and nourish this barren soil. The fruits and flowers may once more spring from it and create life anew. Some are afraid to dive into the deep. They fear they cannot swim. They must learn to be more flexible, for that is the nature of water itself, whose shape adapts to fit the contours of the container. Our minds should be like that, for in truth there are no limits but those which come from one's own vain imaginings. A swing back to water-consciousness could save us all if it comes in time. One day, we shall walk the earth together, hand in hand through a terrestrial paradise, lapped by a sympathetic sea. But please remember this: it is women especially who can save the world—through conscious understanding—and hope needs an aim. I am a star to guide you. Follow me. You may see me kneeling at the Fountain of Youth, pouring forth the waters of life, for I am not called Aquarius the Waterbearer for nothing. And, with the rising of this age, the waters of life shall flow. The tree of life shall spring from the soil I have nourished, and all shall find the secret of everlasting life. But—follow the star. . .'

The words 'follow the star' were heard to echo through the woodlands.

Philomena was determined to follow that star. But it had risen up in a blaze of glory and drifted away.

The rain continued to pour—relentlessly—and Philomena, unable to quell her mounting anguish, cried to herself: 'I shall follow this stream to the mouth of the sea. For if it were tears that caused it to be, then there must be others who are sad like me.' So she let herself float in the stream's embrace down to the shore where it left her, to pace. Philomena wandered along the sands, feeling lost and alone. On and on she walked. Then, looking down, she paused, for there at her feet lay a shell. Intrigued by its delicate pattern, she picked it up and inspected it. It was shaped like a spiral and tinged flesh-pink. Lit by a moonbeam it glowed as mother-of-pearl. She held it to her ear and listened to the voice of the sea.

'Come!' it said. 'Come play with me! The sky is crying down sheets of rain, so you're not so alone in your love-stricken pain. The clouds may be thick, yet the moon still peeps through. She wants to help make your dreams come true. Upon the crests of my waves she sheds her glimmers and makes them into boats for adventurous swimmers. 'So enter my arms. Don't be afraid. Enjoy my world till your boat is made. For water can be very soothing, you know, to the souls of those in whom it may flow.'

Philomena was entranced. The call was irresistible. She ran down the sands to the brink of the shore and waded and dived through the tempest's roar. She swam through the surface and swam some more.

Down. . . down. . . down. . .

'So this is the bed of the sea,' she thought, as the current carried her along the ocean floor. It caressed and comforted her. Philomena was astounded at the sights that passed her as she drifted: plants so unusual—exotic and colourful—and creatures of many a size and shape. Extraordinary scenes that dazzled her eyes. She was so dazzled, in fact, that she hadn't noticed the fins that now decked her limbs. It was only when she struck a hard pointy thing that she felt their protection. But what was this sharp point? It was, she discovered, a spire. And below it was a cathedral made of brilliant jewels. And then she heard them: the faint strains of a choral symphony. The voices were tiny, yet at the same time full, joyful.

As she floated through the open door of the tiny cathedral, the singing turned to laughter. And now she could see them, all gathered in circular formation to greet her: a ring of merry mermaids! They were giggling and laughing and dancing as their hair waved with the waters and their tails gaily flapped. Their laughter rang with melody, in tune with the ocean's harmony. With voices fine as harp-strings, and in a language new, yet understood by Philomena, they invited her to join them. How could she refrain? In the very womb of the sea she dwelt—for who knows how long? For she had been washed of her sorrows. And many a strange and beautiful thing they showed her, such as can only be found by mermaids of the underwater-world. Meanwhile, far across the land, on a cliff-top high above the ocean, a glimmering light, like a beacon in a lighthouse, could be seen through the teeming rain. It was a huge white tower, set against a stormy sea. And, standing on the topmost balcony, illuminated, was an old man with a long white beard—and with blue eyes, blue as the sea on a sunny day. But today his eyes were grey, for they mirror the sea, you see, and today it was windswept and stormy.

He was gazing out at the tossing waves, marvelling at their majesty and power—and at the thousands of little moonbeam boats. 'Indeed the gods move in passion', he murmured to himself, his gnarled fingers clutching the shimmering balcony. 'Perhaps she will come tonight', he said, sadly but hopefully. 'For I know she loves nights like this. We must meet again. For it has been a long time. I wonder, if she comes, which boat she'll be in?' And for a moment his eyes were once more blue, despite his grey surroundings, for at that moment they mirrored a memory. In one of the little boats, a small, green elfin figure with a mane of wild yellow hair and dripping green fins, pranced delightfully through the waves. Around her body was a wild yellow aura—a petal of light, a pure drop of golden fire. Her lightness had taken her out of her element and yet she had survived. When the winds were blowing like tonight she felt most at home. For when the gods moved, the waves and the winds whipped the air into spirals through which she could travel. This she could quite easily acquaint with the ceaseless activity of her flaming origins. And now, having explored the reaches beyond those of a normal child of the flame, Philomena began to feel a freedom she'd never before known. It was as though she had let go—of everything. She felt light, so light, as though whatever or wherever her destiny lay, she would simply be lifted up and transported there. Yes, it was almost as though she was being carried by a trusted yet unknown force—a powerful yet gentle force, which seemed to come from both within and without her. She knew the ways of the waves and sang a song of the sea to steer her frail craft where she wanted. She was well protected by the overhanging ridges of the waves above. Flecks of sea-foam cast a fine net against the sky. Then, looking down, she saw that the waves were rolling up against a solid rock. So she tethered her moonbeam boat to a jut on its edge, stood up, stretched, shook her fins, and proclaimed loudly: 'Fins, be wings! Take me where I must go! I speak with the power of the elements and I ask the angel of air to lend me assistance.' Whereupon the little green fins dried and started to grow. And their sharp little spines turned into long and beautiful feathers.

'How delightful!' Philomena exclaimed, looking at them admiringly. 'Wait till I tell the mermaids about this!' Then she started flapping them gently, and a gust of wind arose to encourage her. 'Flap harder', it seemed to say, 'and when you are in harmony with me I shall take you wherever you desire.' So Philomena flapped and flapped, and, lo and behold! The marvellous green and gold wings lifted her up the side of the cliff and she arrived at the top, hardly believing she was there. The wind howled and whistled around her, and for a moment she was almost blown off the edge. But a few more flaps soon fixed that.

This was most strange, this place in which she now found herself. It was so hard beneath her tiny feet. Her small toes poked inquisitively at the strange rough surface beneath them. 'How very odd! This is not at all like anywhere else I've been,' she thought.

And then she noticed something else: clumps of grass and small bushes flattened by the wind parted to reveal solid white blocks, one on top of the other, leading up a hill. Something told her this is where she should go, but Philomena did not like the feel of these steps and much preferred the springy green grass at the sides, for, being green herself, she felt in harmony with it.

Suddenly, she felt inspired to dance and leap about on the grass. So she leapt and twirled in time to the winds and waves and danced all the way up to the top until she came to the tower. It was so tall that it seemed to be leaning and swaying, but it was hard to tell, for the turret could barely be glimpsed through the clouds. Perhaps it was just the clouds that were moving and not the tower. Yet it did seem to lean and sway. As a tree sways in the breeze, solidly rooted to the earth in which it is grounded, it is swaying and undulating in its upper reaches. 'This tower seems to be more flexible than most,' thought Philomena. 'I wonder who lives here?' In front of the tower, still dancing, she almost bumped into a large silver disc which seemed to be suspended from the clouds, but in fact came from the top of the tower. She beat upon it with her little green hands and beautiful silken sounds made music with the winds. 'How wonderful!' she exclaimed, leaping for joy, dancing and whirling to the toll of the bell upon the grass at the foot of the tower. Again she struck the gong. This time Philomena perceived, much to her surprise, a little archway in the side of the tower, through which she knew she must pass, and had indeed gained right. She passed through the archway and found herself standing at the foot of a spiral staircase. She was bathed in luminous red as she ascended slowly the crystal steps. The red suffused into translucent orange. Stepping higher, she was bathed in sunny yellow-of-the fire, from whence she had sprung. As she spiralled higher, the yellow softened and mellowed into glorious green—the colour she had become. Higher still, and an ethereal blue light pervaded her very being. Then she stepped higher, where the crystal was so fine she felt as though she was enclosed in a bubble of blue light, like a blue pearl, more beautiful than any she had found beneath the waves. This blue pearl was within her. She had only to merge with it and it was all about her as well. It was the most precious jewel she could ever hope to imagine. When she floated up the landing in her blue bubble, the old man saw her. She reached out. He took her little blue hand and kissed it. Then he handed her a wonderful violet flower with a thousand petals—petals of violet light. And as she looked at him again through the shroud of violet, she saw that he was no longer an old man, but eternally youthful, for such is the reward for the brave and strong who, through sufferings and joys, surrender their all. He had dark hair, like gorgeous snakes, honeyed skin, rosy cheeks, and large violet eyes. He was so golden he was almost transparent, except for the snakes which were blue-black, like the darkest hour before the dawn and had iridescent blue scales and whose tongues flickered like flames. Together they were in their blue pearl, the snake-god and the golden–green girl from the flameflower, surrounded by the white light of the tower. Is it this light, illuminating them, which turns the blue of the bubble from translucent to clear, causing Philomena and her knight to appear chameleon–like, as their colours brighten and change, so many glorious hues, beaming out in the fullness of their embrace? Or are these colours simply the language of a love which yearns to express itself?

Whatever, they are propelled—to rise, to soar beyond the clouds, the bubble stretching with them, becoming thinner and thinner until—it is gone, blue into blue. For blue is the backdrop against which the two beings, floating from their embrace are seen—flying. Two birds—wings outstretched—in full flight, in high flight. Here, now, in full view, they are swooping down, as though having a conversation in mid-air, facing one another. They are unlike any bird that is normally seen about the skies in this age and clime. One has a large beak and a curved body like a ballerina: the wings stretched up, arched gracefully, as though gesturing to the other bird while flying. This bird is sleek and blue. The other is more ruffled, with feathers somewhat like ostrich plumes and wings and tail outspread in a fan shape, slightly reminiscent of a peacock's tail when fully spread. The wings are pointed downwards, like the edges of a fan—and the head is raised, with a beautiful swan-like curve to it, though the neck is not so long.

But the shapes these birds describe as they dance in the air! For that is what they are doing as they spiral and swirl, tracing visual echoes of delight. The feathers of the second bird are of an amazing hue and design. They are edged in gold with strange hieroglyphic figures in dark green at their centre. So that, when the bird moves, strange, shimmering shekel-type designs are formed in space. While its iridescent blue companion, sleek as a seal, provides a stunning contrast. It is as though they form a pas de deux, with the blue sky as backdrop. Whoever it was said that it was only birds of a feather that flock together had not seen these two, for each is unique, though they fly as one. They are drawn in their flight towards a giant pyramid upon which they are now performing. It has a circular balcony on top, balanced at the very tip of the pyramid, the prime spot. It's almost like being in the balcony at the opera – for those lucky enough to be perched in this 'box–seat', for the balcony is transparent, though the pyramid is not. Balanced as it is at the tip, it is in direct alignment with the pyramid's axis.

There are figures in the balcony. They cannot be seen, yet their presence is felt, watching the ballet of the birds. It is as if the whole ballet is taking place on an ethereal plane, and the two beings are somehow connected with those buried within the pyramid. It is as though they had once risen in a long line of light, ascending the very core of the pyramid—and had now risen through the balcony at the top—to issue forth and share the fruits of their transformation, their splendour in unison.

They have definitively human characteristics. Their wings have the gestures of arms and their bodies arch like the human torsos of trained dancers. Their movements are explicit. The way they ruffle their feathers, like luxurious costumes in full display upon a floodlit stage—the most floodlit stage you could ever imagine! Without limit! And from the magnificent circular balcony quite fascinating sights may be seen, if one has time to see before joining in the dance, for here the definitions are blurred. Space is not defined in the same way as on a normal stage …

Performer and audience… substance transmutes. The audience is diving off the balcony, to spread their wings perhaps.

But the pyramid guards its secret. Only the birds can tell, yet they prefer to dance it. That way more can be made known and lines of light can be drawn in space for those who have eyes to see.

Pregnant and heavy with life at its zenith
the moon is beaming her radiance
upon the earth below
to reveal from her centre
a sparkling jewel
a treasure indeed.
Here at her heart
glows the scarlet fan
and upon the fan
engraved in silver
are two dancing figures
frozen in a moment of ecstasy
silver upon red upon white.
Such is the image-flash
transmitted by the moon in her state of fullness
a moment transitory yet indelible.
For the figures
silver as the stars
are etched in the archives of eternity.
The moon is shining forth in all her majesty.
It is as though she is bedecked in her full regal splendour
the robes of royalty
as befitting the Queen of Night.
And all the stars dance in her attendance
while the earth below is a-flower with sparks
shooting skyward for all to see:
a glorious fountain of flame
trickling filaments of bliss
like fragments of falling stars.

"It's imagination that chains us and it's imagination that sets us free."

(Venus)

MELODY LEMOND
melodylemond@gmail.com
www.melodylemond.com

www.scarletfan.com.au

Also by Melody Lemond:

Sea Moon
A Collection of Poem Shapes
www.poemshapes.com

GAILY RUSSELL
Artist
gailyday@gmail.com